T0199122

Mallory of the Angels 2

Planet Las Nuves

C A R L O S   T .   L E O N

WESTBOW
P R E S S®
A DIVISION OF THOMAS NELSON
& ZONDERVAN

Copyright © 2017 Carlos T. Leon.

Cover by Michael Alicea

All rights reserved. No part of this book may be used or reproduced by any means,
graphic, electronic, or mechanical, including photocopying, recording, taping or by
any information storage retrieval system without the written permission of the author
except in the case of brief quotations embodied in critical articles and reviews.

This is a work of fiction. All of the characters, names, incidents, organizations, and dialogue
in this novel are either the products of the author's imagination or are used fictitiously.

WestBow Press books may be ordered through booksellers or by contacting:

WestBow Press
A Division of Thomas Nelson & Zondervan
1663 Liberty Drive
Bloomington, IN 47403
www.westbowpress.com
1 (866) 928-1240

Because of the dynamic nature of the Internet, any web addresses or links contained
in this book may have changed since publication and may no longer be valid. The views
expressed in this work are solely those of the author and do not necessarily reflect the views
of the publisher, and the publisher hereby disclaims any responsibility for them.

Any people depicted in stock imagery provided by Thinkstock are models,
and such images are being used for illustrative purposes only.
Certain stock imagery © Thinkstock.

ISBN: 978-1-5127-5811-5 (sc)
ISBN: 978-1-5127-5810-8 (e)

Library of Congress Control Number: 2016915865

Print information available on the last page.

WestBow Press rev. date: 12/12/2016

CONTENTS

CHAPTER ONE - THE CITIZENS OF LAS NUVES:

Las Nuves is a planet consisting of 5 billion people, With the turmoil existing on Earth, His Son Jesus about to be crucified, and Lucifer creating havoc on Earth, God decided to create several new planets, each with a form of life resembling Human Beings. Each planet will mature at an accelerated rate of growth, but each maturing at different times. The people of each new planet will enjoy the right to choose right from wrong as God gave to the people of Earth.

The women of Las Nuves have an almost indescribable beauty. 98% of the women grow to be very tall, slender and extremely beautiful. Their eyes are the same colors as those of the people who come from Earth. Their hair is straight and long, reaching past their knees. Their faces are flawless and use only a hint of organic flowers, plants, and trees to highlight and enhance their natural beauty.

The women can be rough and rugged, but they choose to be soft and gentile. The art of cooking and taking care of a family is introduced to the girls at age 10. Prior to age 10, the girls go to school and are allowed to play until they get exhausted. Women in Las Nuves are allowed to choose their own husbands and the marriages usually last a life time. In general, the women in Las Nuves are happy and are very well taken care of. The women of Las Nuves tend to greet each other as sisters rather then neighbors. There is an equal ratio of men to women. Almost all women marry and the typical family consists of a husband, wife, and eight children. Las Nuves families will take care of each other, their elderly, and any citizen who can no longer take care of themselves, whether they are family or not. The men of Las Nuves grow up to 8 feet tall by the time they are 16 years of age. They are muscular and extremely strong . At 10, they are taught how to take care of a family and how to gather and grow food. Also at age 10, the boys are presented with a variety of occupations, of which they will select two occupations. They are then expected to become skilled and expert workers. Since Las Nuves has never seen war, no army is needed to protect their way of life, therefore military service is not one of the occupational choices given to young men. Life in Las Nuves is very peaceful and boys are taught to be friendly and respectful of others. Avoiding conflicts and hurting or injuring others is strictly enforced by the parents and the Priests. These boys are also taught the sanctity of marriage and the blessings of being a part of a family.

For both boys and girls the teaching of God and God's blessings begin as soon as they can speak and continue throughout their entire lifetime. Children learn that through God and His goodness, Las Nuves receives peace, plenty of food and water, excellent weather, strength, and all good things that Las Nuves now enjoys.

The children are taught that through God everything is possible and that Las Nuves is one of God's special creations. Everyone in Las Nuves knows that God is love and that God loves them unconditionally.

Las Nuves has only one religion and only one God. To keep the faith and the teaching in this religion, 100,000 Priests are elected to maintain the temples and continue to teach the word of God. These elected Priests will then elect two Supreme Priests, one Supreme Priest for each of their two continents, with their ultimate responsibility to communicate with God and present God's word to the Priests and the people.

Since the planet Las Nuves is twice the size of Earth and less populated, each individual in Las Nuves has plenty of space to enjoy all that life has to offer them. Las Nuves has two continents, each separated by a large ocean of fresh water. The people of Las Nuves considered their planet as God's greatest creation. The weather is always comfortable with temperatures varying from 70 degrees (F) TO 85 degrees (F). There is a light sprinkle of rain each day at approximately 3 p.m. lasting only 35 minutes. During those 35 minutes, the skies would be filled with magnificent rainbows that could be seen in both continents. Las Nuves is a very green planet which allowed for perfect growing and planting grounds. The soil is truly fertile allowing for plants and vegetables to grow fresh and tall with minimum work required on the part of the people. The food produced by the farmers can feed the people of Las Nuves three times over. The planet is the birth place of so many types of flowers, bushes, and trees that the people considered it a living Oasis. Las Nuves has soft beautiful clouds consisting of light pastel colors of light blue, mild pink, and fluffy white. The planet is named after these beautiful clouds. The entire population of Las Nueves spoke the same Language, similar to American English. Because of the warm sun shining 16 hours a day, most of the people are light brown to light red in color. By their own nature, the people are a friendly, gregarious people who got along with each other extremely well. There is no discrimination in Las Nuves, as each person is created equal and is allowed to choose his way of life, so long as it did not interfere with others. There were extremely few cases or times when a dispute arose among the citizens. The people of Las Nuves are truly happy with the life God has given them. God is an integral part of their daily lives. Each section of the cities elected their own Priest to keep them in line with the teaching of God. These Priests take their assignment to represent their section of people very seriously. The Priests then elect a Supreme Priest for each of the continents. These Supreme Priests enjoyed total loyalty of the Priesthood and the citizens of Las Nuves. The people enjoyed a wonderful life because God is always there for them and in turn, they are there for God. The only religion practiced on Las Nuves is to worship God as the True God. The religion called for following all of God's edicts presented to them by their Supreme Priest and/or members of the Priesthood. Besides the two Supreme Priests, there are 100,000 elected Priests, half from each continent. The religion called for the citizens to elect their Priests to represent them in all matters regarding the word of God. Being a Priest is one of the greatest honors that any citizen can hope for in Las Nuves.

The 100,000 priests will then be responsible for electing their spiritual leaders, their Supreme Priest. These Supreme Priests are both the religious and the government leaders of the planet. Their words are treated as if God himself is speaking. It is truly a very powerful position. It is known for centuries that when God has a message for the people of Las Nuves, God will speak to the Supreme Priests who will then pass the message on to the Priests who will then inform the people. This style of religion keep the citizens very close to God and allowed God to be in their daily lives. Las Nuves did not know war, but it did contain a police style defense force to protect against wild animals or to settle disputes peacefully. The police force is not a military force. It is not trained for war or for major conflicts. The police force consisted of 50,000 police officers in each of the two continents for a combine police force of 100,000 policemen. The police force come under the supervision and command of the Supreme Priests.

CHAPTER TWO - LOVE, PEACE, PROSPERITY:

For thousands of years, the people of Las Nuves were content and giving God his accolades. They never wavered from their devotion to God and were grateful for the Priests that kept God's will at all times. There is love in their works, there is love in their accomplishments, there is love for each other, and there is a great love for their families. Love is the force behind the greatness of Las Nuves. With love came prosperity beyond compare. Each family is able to support themselves and assist others who either by injury or illness, can not go to work. It is indeed a God's paradise. Peace abounded everywhere. The people of Las Nuves are happy and very proud of their status with God. Due to the fact that peace and love is paramount, there are very few squabbles, fights, or disagreements. Children are taught to respect the rights of others and to play without hurting or causing pain. The children grow strong, both physically and emotionally. Yet, with all this happiness, somewhere in the hierarchy of the Priesthood, a voice of discontent began to speak. A voice not at all happy with God or God's power over the people. A voice that wants to bring discontent to Las Nuves. A voice that wants to bring down the love of God and all his goodness. An unhappy jealous voice.

CHAPTER THREE - UNHOLY PRIEST GUNGULAE:

Unknown to many in the sect of Priests, the Supreme Priest from the larger of the two continents, named Supreme Priest Gungulae, decided to prove that he is as powerful as God and can even do a better job of running the planet without God's help. Secretly, for the past two years, Gungulae began to "wine and dine" several of the influential members of the Priesthood with the purpose of winning their vote in any religious matter or any non religious matter that He, Supreme Priest Gungulae, will present or recommend. Gungulae already enjoyed nearly 90 percent following of the 100,000 Priests of both continents. Even the other Supreme Priest Esteban, of the smaller continent, yields to Gungulae the majority of time, mainly during maters of religion. The majority of the Priests' believed that Gungulae has a strong tie to God and that God favors him over all the other Priests in current standing. At this moment, Gungulae is the most powerful man in Las Nuves. Gungulae, an intelligent leader and statesman, realize that it will not take much to swing the planet to his way of thinking. Gungulae has been ruling the planet for 30 years, and other than praying to God, Gungulae did not see where God gave him any specific advise on how to run the planet or how to improve the welfare of the citizens. All the improvements and betterment came as a result of his, Gungulae's own efforts and direction. He has no need for God since God no longer exists in his mind. Being the most powerful man in Las Nuves, his position dictates that he is greater and more powerful than God. With each day that passes, Gungulae believe deeply that his cause to replace God is the best thing for Las Nuves. How to achieve this mission? That is a very big question. First he has to establish a plan and get loyal subjects both in the Priesthood and in the populace of Las Nueves. Gungulae has a genius brain and a taste for power. This combination will give him all he needs to succeed. Succeed he will, without doubt and without God.

First, before he established his plan, Gungulae must continue with giving favors to those Priest and people of power and influence. In today's world, the people are happy and paying less attention to the messages from God. Gungulae has helped create this lack of interest by just keeping them in the dark and not mentioning God as often as he has done in the recent past.

Second, Gungulae must give orders to his most loyal subjects to create situations that will cause the people to suffer pain, be injured, or die, then link these horrible events to the will of God.

Third, Gungulae must build a secret military style army of loyal supporters to control or punish those who object to his power.

Forth, Gungulae must find a way to eliminate Supreme Priest Esteban from power and leave him as the only leader of the planet.

CHAPTER FOUR - WHY HAS GOD FORSAKEN US?

On the smaller continent, there are 125 major cities containing 1.5 billion people living within their boundaries. The fresh water is transported to the cities via highways of aqueducts after being purified from the fresh water oceans. Water is plentiful and as it is in all other planets, water is life giving. The drinking waters of Las Nuves is sweet, clear, and very refreshing. These aqueducts, although old in years, are meticulous maintained and are up to complete safety standards for strength, easy flowing, and free of impurities. Any country in any world will be proud to have such a smooth working aqueduct. There are approximately 10,000 workers assigned to each aqueduct system in each continent. The aqueduct workers keep the pumps updated and make sure the highways of aqueducts are free of holes and obstacles. Over all, each continent has one major aqueduct with hundreds of tributaries that helped the water to keep flowing smoothly. The builders of the aqueduct built nothing less than a miracle and a wonder of Las Nuves. With out any warning, large sections of the main aqueduct cracked and caused the purified water to spill into the countryside. These cracks are large enough to stop 90% of the water from reaching the cities and the citizens. This has not happened before in the history of the aqueduct, causing many of the city leaders and Priests to ask questions as to what has occurred. The loss of their daily water supply caused for the first time, anger and arguments among the people. Unknown to many leaders and Priest, Gungulae had planted people loyal to him to create anger and to cause dissention among the populace. Gungulae has just started his first of many evil schemes in progress. The trouble makers planted by Gungulae, as per his orders, began to ask questions of their Priests as to what happened to the aqueducts and who was to bare the blame. The Priests, of course requested audiences with the Supreme Priests for answers. As in previous matters, Supreme Priest Esteban, of the smaller continent gave way to Gungulae for the answers. The angry people planted by Gungulae are asking why God will allow such a horror to occur. Seizing his opportunity to blame God and to get the people of Las Nuves to believe God no longer favored them, Gungulae immediately let it be known that God is upset with the people of Las Nuves. Gungulae stated that God told him that the people are not working hard enough to please Him and that the people are not paying their just dues to the Priests. Gungulae immediately placed several thousand of his Priests to repair the aqueduct, which they did quickly. Water is restored and the people of the 125 cities. The word is then passed around that it was through Gungulae's love and generosity that the aqueducts were fixed quickly and the possible harm kept to a minimum. The people of Las Nuves are not yet ready to believe that God disliked them. Yet, the people thanked Gungulae and his Priests for saving their lives. **The first bad seed has been planted.**

Two weeks after the failure of the aqueducts, a caravan of 300 school children was traveling over a country bridge that led to a holy shrine available to the public. This bridge has been used thousands of times before and was known to be in good working order and properly maintained. Again, without ay warning, the side of the bridge fell down causing the caravan to fall sideways and send the children tumbling to the ground. Nearly 200 children were seriously injured, with 25 in critical condition. Again, agents planted by Gungulae began to ask angry questions as to who is at fault in this tragedy. They asked the priests if God is also responsible for this tragedy as well?

CHAPTER FIVE - MORE PAIN, MORE BLAME.

As it just happened to be, there are several hundred medically trained Priests within minutes of the accidental bridge collapse. As instructed by Gungulae, these trained Priest are able to care for the injured children and avoid loss of life or permanent disfigurement. Known to only a very few selected Priests and a few city leaders, Gungulae had set up the bridge to collapse and also to have the medical Priests available immediately on site. Once again, when the questions came in from the angry parents, Gungulae is pleased to give them the answer as to who was to blame. Gungulae, expressing sorrow and piety, stated that when he asked

God for the reason, God informed him that the people of Las Nuves are in disfavor for their lack of respect of God and for failing to keep the God's word. This is the 2nd event in two weeks that caused concern and pain to the people of Las Nuves. With Gungulae placing the blame on God and with Gungulae and his Priests being on the spot to help the people, shades of doubt began to appear in the minds of many of the people of Las Nuves. It seemed to these people that it was Gungulae who has their welfare and safety in mind. **A second bad seed has been planted**.

The population of the large continent also suffered sever setbacks. Somehow and unexpectedly, over 90% of the best planting fields became polluted with a green slime that smothered the growing plants and would not let any of the planted food grow. The farmers, who took pride in being able to feed their world, became scared and concerned that they will be blamed for this tragedy. If this evil is not corrected, a famine would quickly occur and that will bring untold misery and starvation to the people of Las Nuves. By now, the people of Las Nuves are used to calling on Supreme Priest Gungulae for his advice and for his ability to repair the situation. The people requested Gungulae's help and as usual, Gungulae, with the help of the Priesthood, cleaned up the green slime and saved the food stock, saved the land, saved the farmers, and saved the people of Las Nuves. These evil occurrences are kept a secret from the populace, and again, Gungulae has instructed his Priests trained in chemistry to create a ferocious looking slime that could be cleaned up quickly. Now, when the questions were asked as to why such a possible disaster could occurred, Gungulae, with somewhat of an angry tone, stated that God was unhappy with the people of Las Nuves and will abandon them if the people will not comply with his teaching and directions. Gungulae has been informed by God that the worst was yet to come if the people did not increase their tidings to the Priesthood, that is, paying 70% more in contributions. Gungulae told the people that God is angry with Gungulae for correcting the turmoil that God created for Las Nuves and that he, Gungulae should not interfere again. Gungulae said he stood his ground with God and told God that he will not allow God to continue to hurt or destroy the people of Las Nuves. He told God that He, Gungulae, is honored to be the champion of the people of Las Nuves. **A third bad seed had been planted**.

After hearing that God is about to desert them and cause them more harm than good, the leading Priest, Supreme Priest Esteban, and the leaders of the people demanded action be taken to save the planet from the evils of God. The Priest and the People demanded unity in facing the challenges of God and unity in the leadership of Las Nuves, and presenting only one voice against their bad God.

In a vote to unite the Priesthood, Esteban, resigned his post of Supreme Priest of the Smaller continent and voted that all the power of the Priesthood should be in the hands of one man, and that one man is Gungulae. The vote was unanimous with 90,000 Priest and 3.5 billion people voting for Gungulae to be the" King Priest" of Las Nuves. With his new post secured and with the people of Las Nuves no longer happy with the way God has brought destruction to their land, Gungulae will now concentrate on forming his army to maintain the control he now won legally. 'I am greater than God" yelled King Priest Gungulae.

CHAPTER SIX - MY ARMY - MY POWER - MY WAY:

True to his word, Gungulae established a standing army of 5 million soldiers plus his 90,000 personal guard consisting of the former Priests. Gungulae has the sole power to talk and negotiate with God. The former 10,000 Priests who did not vote for him and the 1.5 million people who also did not vote for him, and of course, God, are now going to be the target of his anger.

Gungulae made it possible for his personal guard and his soldiers to get the best of everything and that they get it first. These men are allowed to take whatever they wanted from the 1.5 billion people with no questions asked. The power yielded by his troops is mesmerizing. Torture is now rampant. Any citizen who did not move quickly to an order from the soldiers or personal guards are subjected to torture or imprisonment. The citizens soon realized that the life they had under God's embrace is far better than whatever Gungulae has given them. These pople have remained true to God and did not believe all that Gungulae had told them about God. No matter, they are powerless against Gungulae and his army. How to stop Gungulae? No one knew the answer. What was once a beautiful God loving planet has turned into an evil waste of a God-less land with God-less leaders. The people of Las Nuves started to realize that it was not God who deserted them, but that they themselves had deserted God. And all it took to lose it all was to believe in the falsehood of Gungulae. These few pople knew that something has to be done and quickly.

The questions now are how to get in contact with God, restore His faith in the people, and how to convince the people of Las Nuves that Gungulae is the evil source of their misery, not God. Convincing the people will be difficult, as 90% were taking whatever they wanted with no repercussion. Gungulae has a very strong hold over the people and the more power he gives to the people, the more power is wanted to control other people.

CHAPTER SEVEN - A HUMBLE MAN:

What is also needed is a person with a strong belief in God, a person who has not compromised his allegiance to God, and a person who will be willing to overcome the mountains of obstacles he will have to face in accepting the challenge to defeat King Priest Gungulae and his followers.

The people who did not vote for Gungulae to be King Priest are always under constant observation. They are placed in Jail for any infraction of the laws established by Gungulae. Those who strongly objected to Gungulae's law are severely beaten, tortured, and in many cases, sentenced to death without a traial. The majority of objectors learned to keep their opinions to themselves while living in the cities and whenever possible, escape to several caves that are rarely visited and basically unknown to the people who mainly lived within the walls of the cities. Life in the caves is difficult, but the pople who escaped to these caves find that they were free to worship God without reprisals. There is plenty of food and enough food to maintain several million people in each of the giant caves throughout the planet. In the past, city dwellers did not like to leave the cities and did not investigate the caves and the empty valleys that surrounded the cities. It is believed by the city people that bad things happened to anyone who wondered in the caves. A former Priest from the big continent named Jomax felt deeply that God is calling to him to stop the pain of the people of Las Nuves. Jomax is a very strong young man, eight feet tall, muscular in build, yet gentle, and humble of heart and spirit. It was he who braved the forces of Gungulae by sneaking in food and medicines to the cave people. Soon, with an additional 500 former Priests, he began to build a small but efficient army that will be able to take on and defeat small patrols of Gungulae's forces.

Always thinking and seeking out information, Jomax is able to contact the former Supreme Priest Esteban and convince him to join him and help the people of the caves. Esteban agreed and with the combination of Jomax and Esteban, a line of communication with God was once again established.

Chapter eight - Spreading the word:

Jomax sends all the former Priests into each city of both continents. While at the cities, each Priest is to carefully spread the word that Gungulae used lies and deception to blame God for all the wrong that befell Las Nuves. In addition, the priest are to recruit individuals who will be willing to spy for them and keep the cave Priests informed on what is taking place in the cities.

The cave Priests are to spread word of hope and a return of God to Las Nuves. The Priest are also to spread the word that there is room for anyone who wants to escape the cities and move into the caves. If their choice is to move to the caves, they are to bring anything of value, food, and medical supplies. The cave Priests explained how to get to the nearest cave where were help is available and where they can then be transferred to a larger cell.

After 5 years of Gungulae's rule, a great number of people who voted for him to become King Priest, began to feel the strain of being unfaithful to God and to themselves. If these people began to speak their mind against all the wrong that is now taking place, Gungulae's forces will arrest and punish them into submission. Gungulae is not only getting stronger in power, but the people soon learned that it is going to be his way or go to his death camps where people are worked and tortured until they collapsed and died. Gungulae has the force of the army to command fear, respect, and obedience from the people. The more and continued punishment is dealt to the people. the more and more people begin to see through Gungulae's lies, and more and more people begin to pray for God intervene and restore Las Nuves to the level of love it enjoyed while God existed in their lives. Gungulae, with his powerful army, made sure that God is not openly mentioned in any conversation, or written in any text. To speak of God is to be sentenced to death. It soon came to pass that being sent to the death camps is a better option than living under the rule of Gungulae. Gungulae is not troubled or bothered at all by the suffering of the people. He has proved to the people of Las Nuves that he can succeed in ruling Las Nuves without the help of God. He again proclaimed proudly, "I am now, and will always be, greater than God".

CHAPTER NINE - CLIMBING THE MOUNTAINS:

King Priest Gungulae gets word of the underground cave movement. He also finds out about the renegade cave Priests that are trying to undermine his rule. "If it's a fight they want, a fight they will get" declared Gungulae. His orders are swift and to the point. Arrest all Priests that are not already aligned with me. Then arrest all persons who did not vote for me to become King Priest. These rebels are to be treated as traitors and anyone of them who defies an order to turn themselves in will be shot on sight. The order to shoot these traitors will also include shooting each member of their family as well. As the order went out, Jomax and his Priests laid out a plan to sneak the people out from the cities and bring them into the caves. The soldiers of Gungulae's army, not knowing where the caves are located, will have a difficult time finding them. So between midnight and just prior to day break, Jomax's men had captured, tied and gagged the guards at the gates. Quickly and as quietly as possible, Jomax's men removed all the people, who are under orders to be shot, out of the cities and into the caves. The plans for evacuation went perfectly without delays or disruption. The people, knowing that their lives and the lives of their children are at stake, moved quietly and efficiently with the minimum of noise. The plan, very well thought out by Jomax, worked to perfection. Now to keep the people safe, well fed, and have plenty of water available to drink.

Gungulae was furious. "Who could think of a plan like that? Who would have the nerve to carry it out? Where were my guards while the people were being moved"? So many questions and not so many answers. Looking at the good side of this situation, King Priest Gungulae noted that at least the dissenters and troublemakers are out of the cities with very little to eat, and less water to drink. Soon they will give up and return to his rule. Yes, that's exactly what they will do. Then I will know who their leader is and give

him my full attention. Hurting and destroying him will be very gratifying. First, to make an example of the guards who allowed the exodus to occur. The task now for Jomax is not only serious and critical, but failure now will be the end of life for these people and without doubt, the end of life for Las Nuves as well. Jomax, Esteban, and the cave Priests all got down on their knees and began to pray. Each prayer asking for God's forgiveness and His Divine intervention. Within moments, the entire population in the caves joined them in prayers.

CHAPTER TEN - GUNGULAE GOES ON THE OFFENSIVE:

King Priest Gungulae takes personal charge of his army. First, all the rebels on the small continent will be wiped out and totally destroyed. Four of his best military divisions will leave the cities and search and destroy all caves and all persons living within the caves. There will be no quarter given. Any person found outside the cities is to be declared an enemy of Gungulae and destroyed immediately. Fortunately, while praying for God's forgiveness, Jomax and Esteban, both received messages from God stating: "to survive and save the people of the small continent, many ships would have to be built or obtained so the people can be moved to the larger continent's cave where safety, shelter, food, and water will be available for these large number of people fleeing Gungulae's armies.

There in the larger continent, the people will have unity and strength to stop Gungulae's military advances until God's plan of retribution and salvation can be presented." As the 500,000 soldiers spread out over the uninhibited lands and cave sites of the small continent, not one person is found. The caves have been deserted for more than 10 days and the fire coals are cold and dry. The military leaders could not believe their eyes. How can so many millions of people just disappear with a trace or evidence as to where they went to. Notifying Gungulae will be very difficult, but reporting the findings is a must do task. Gungulae, upon hearing the news that the caves on the small continent were empty, began a house to house search in every city of the small continent believing that the people returned to the cities while his armies were out looking for them in the caves. He can not imagine any other way millions of people could disappear from sight. Yet, the search turned out nothing but people still loyal to him. This situation is not good. He must find out soon what happened or lose control of his army and his power. This He will not permit. Somewhere there are answer. He will have to be smarter and open with his thinking. "Rebels"! Finding the rebels is now a top priority throughout Las Nuves.

CHAPTER ELEVEN - GUNGULAE SETS HIS TRAP:

Despite a safe landing on the large continent of Las Nuves, Jomax and the people are spotted by a lone soldier on patrol near the ocean water purifying plants. Soldiers rarely left the city and this soldier is assigned to guard the water purification plant. Taking a break from his station, the soldier had walked along the shores and by chance, noticed many ships landing on the coast line. Staying unseen, he followed Jomax and the people to the large caves. He is not sure what is happening, but upon being relieved, he presented his finding to his superior, who immediately took the soldier directly to King Priest Gungulae's official office.

Gungulae gave permission for the soldier and his superior officer to enter his chambers. The soldier detailed his observations and findings in a truly military style report. The soldier left nothing out detailing the ship landings to the movement towards the cave, and most important, that a former Priest named Jomax is the leader. He also noted that former Supreme Priest Esteban is also part of the rebels, but he did not know in what capacity he served.

For his important findings and report, Gungulae promoted the soldier to rank of captain and gave his family priority in shopping for food and supplies. Needless to say, the soldier left the meeting with Gungulae more devoted and extremely loyal to his King Priest. Finding the rebels is very good news indeed. Calling in his generals and high ranking Priests, Gungulae initiated his plan, to trap the rebels, and totally destroy them and their leaders once and for all. The plan is three fold. One, to have his military army surround the caves and keep the rebels inside and keep them from escaping. Two, his own personal guards consisting of Priests, will remain in the cities to protect him and the temples. Three, with part one and part two of the plan in place, He, Gungulae, will personally come over to the cave sites and offer the rebel leaders his proposals of surrender. The complete surrender will allow the people to return to the cities with no punishment or jail time. There will be a limited time to worship God if they so desired. The cave people will have a say in the government and have representatives that they themselves elect. Of course, this is in no way truthful. Gungulae has already given his orders that the moment the cave people accepted his proposal and laid down their arms, the complete slaughter and destructions of these cave people will begin.

Chapter twelve - The enemies at our gates:

The out-post sentry in the largest cave reported to Jomax that a very large movement of troops and supplies is moving very rapidly from all direction of his line of sight and heading towards the caves. The near-post sentry is now also reporting at least 8 battalions of troops is approaching directly at the front of the main cave. The sentry at the rear-post reports that at least 5 battalions of troops are spreading out behind the caves, mainly behind the main exit of the cave. It appears for the moment that Jomax and his people are surrounded and without hope of escape. Jomax immediately sets up defenses at the entrance and exits of each cave. Escape is not part of Jomax's plan. Surrender is also not in his plan, Each member of the cave people knows that victory or defeat will start and end right here at the caves. Esteban started a prayer and every member inside the caves joined in the prayer. If they are to die, let it be dying believing in God. Jomax, understanding the burden of leadership, tried to prepare himself mentally and physically. This is going to be a very long day and night. His people have enough food and water to sustain a siege of at least 30 days.. Enough medical supplies to last at least 25 days of fierce fighting. Jomax can not tell how long the siege or the fight will last, only that he has to be there for the people and for Esteban who gave up everything to come back to the graces of God. At high noon, Gungulae and his ambassadors approached the caves to speak with Jomax and Esteban regarding the avoidance of bloodshed and presenting Gungulae's proposal for surrender. The leading ambassador is himself a high ranking army general and with him came 2 captains and a 20 man protection squad. Gungulae came quickly to the point. To receive the promise of no reprisals, "I require a complete surrender of all military trained Priests and civilians. A complete surrender of Jomax, Esteban, and any other recognized leader. All weapons must be placed down at the front of each cave. Everyone, man, woman, and child, will come out with their hands up in the air and head and eyes facing down. No exception will be allowed or tolerated.

CHAPTER THIRTEEN - NO DEAL - NO SURRENDER:

Jomax looked Gungulae and his ambassador directly in their eyes. "We will not accept any part of your proposals". Jomax turned towards his people and told them: "Gungulae is not known for his honesty or for keeping his word". "I suspect you have orders to kill me and Esteban as soon as we surrender to you". "We are free people who believe in God and we will not submit to you, false King Priest of Las Nuves". "Each of us here are willing to die for the right to believe in God, and for the rights of our children to be able to believe in God without being tortured or killed". "Go now and do not return unless it is to tell me that you, Gungulae have surrendered your post of King Priest and have restored God to the top of worship in Las Nuves". Gungulae merely got up, smiled, and said that there will be no other communication until Jomax raised the white flag. "The horror that happens next to your people, Gungulae stated, will happen because of your refusal of my peace proposals". "You have brought destruction upon yourselves". With that, Gungulae, the ambassador, and their escorts left the cave area. Immediately, Jomax set up a defensive perimeter at each cave' entrance and exit. Gungulae's army begins a small campaigned of harassment at each of the caves. Each incursion is a lighting strike and a quick retreat. These attacks are merely to frighten or to find any weakness in the defense of the caves. So far very little damage has been done to either side. In total, there are 16 major or very large caves and 10 medium caves. The larger caves are connected to each other by tunnels but the medium caves are not connected to the larger caves. Therefore, Jomax kept the majority of the people and supplies inside the larger caves. Each medium cave has a means of escape to a larger cave. Gungulae is quick to find this out and used this information to his advantage. He will begin attacking and capturing the medium caves in hopes of causing over crowding in the larger caves. At midnight he attacked the 10 medium caves.

CHAPTER FOURTEEN - GOD HEARS THE PRAYERS:

At the main caves, the fighting can be heard coming from many of the medium caves. The fighting is ferocious and battle cries can be heard from both sides. Jomax knows that at best, he needs to remain in the large cave because that will be the place of the final battle. Once again, he got down on his knees and prayed that God or his angels will hear their prayer and intervene on their behalf. Jomax knows that without God's help, Las Nuves is doomed to be God-less and its beautiful people will perish never knowing the full extent of God's love. By 7 a.m., the fighting at the medium caves had stopped. Gungulae's army had captured 6 of the 10 medium caves. Survivors of the captured caves escaped to the remaining 4 medium caves. Jomax made the decision to abandoned all the medium caves and move those people into the main caves. Within two hours of the people,moving out of the medium caves, smoke and flames can be seen coming out of all the those caves. As it was, luck is still on Jomax's side because the people of the medium caves suffered only minimum casualties and as they fled for safety, they brought all the food, water, medical supplies, and weapons the could carry with them. God is acutely aware of the issues in Las Nuves. He has heard the prayers and the request for intervention. Generally speaking, once God gives the people the right to choose right from wrong, He rarely intervenes.

Yet, He has indeed intervened on Earth several times. God decided that He will send an emissary to Las Nuves to see if the situation there can be corrected and peace and love restored. God decided to send Mallory of the Angels escorted by Angel General Solrac for personal protection. Knowing the prior success of Mallory of the Angels, God was pleased with His selection.

CHAPTER FIFTEEN - THE GREETING - THE DECEPTION:

Mallory of the Angels accepted her new assignment with great expectation. Regarded in Heaven as one of the top diplomats and stateswoman, Mallory of the Angels had, on her first assignment, successfully brought the end of Hell and returned Lucifer back to the Graces of God. Fearless as she is loving, Mallory of the Angels is blessed with the ability to see the entire issue and come up with solutions that will satisfy everyone involved in the dispute. With the instructions given to Her by God, Mallory of the Angels proceeded to Las Nuves accompanied by General Solrac. General Solrac defeated Lucifer in a one on one battle in Hell when Lucifer was unable to continue the fight and surrendered. Lucifer then placed himself in the mercy of God. Consequently, Lucifer was accepted back into Heaven and given the name of Gregorio. The victory over hell and Lucifer is still celebrated in Heaven. Their arrival on Las Nuves is a great sensation, causing all work to stop. Their arrival presented Gungulae both with problems and a plan to completely remove God from Las Nuves forever. First order of business, to invite Mallory of the Angels to his temple and hear what she has to say. So, with great fanfare, Gungulae, with thousands of his Priests dressed in white and pink gowns, escorted Mallory of the Angels and General Solrac into the main temple. Mallory of the Angels immediately stated what she has to say She will say it to both parties of the dispute, i.e., Gungulae, Jomax and Esteban. Mallory of the Angels requested that Gungulae provide a safe escort to Jomax and Esteban so they can attend the meeting. Gungulae was very happy to comply and immediately sent emissaries to the caves to notify Jomax that his presence and that of Esteban is requested at the meeting with God's emissary, Mallory of the Angels.

CHAPTER SIXTEEN - GUNGULAE PLANS A TRAP:

While waiting for Jomax and Estebam to join him in the meeting with God's ambassador, Gungulae began to plot the capture of Mallory of the Angels, her General escort, and least but not last, the capture of Jomax and Esteban. The plan seem so easy. All his enemies will be within his control, surrounded by his Priests, and no help to assist God's ambassadors should they try to escape their capture. With the capture of Jomax and Esteban, the rebels will have no leaders and then they will fall quickly to his army. With the capture of Mallory of the Angels, God will have to concede Las Nuves to Gungulae if he wanted Mallory of the Angels back in heaven. By the end of this day, Gungulae will rule supreme. He licked his lips just like he had a big juicy steak before him. Showing no signs of his evil intent, Gungulae, with the skills of a master showman, began the meeting in grand style fit for kings and queens. Mallory of the Angels sat on the left side of the table, first chair. Next to Her sat General Solrac, dressed in full military dress. Next to Him sat Jomax. Then Esteban sat next to Jomax and finally Jomax's body guard. Opposite Mallory of the Angels sat Gungulae. To his left are the four highest ranking Priests, two from the small continent and two from the large continent. At the head of the tables on both ends stood Gungulae's body guards. Opening up the meeting with greetings and introductions, Gungulae sat back down and allowed Mallory of the Angels to speak first and present God's proposal for peace. She is already aware of the history of Las Nuves, the take over and conversion of the Priesthood from God loving to God hating, and the torture and imprisonment of those who refused to stop believing in God, Mallory of the Angels jumped in with both feet hitting the ground. She immediately set the stage to prove that God had nothing to do with the evils and harm that came upon the people of Las Nuves. In fact, all the evidence will show that the damages are man-made in a deliberate attempt to blame God.

CHAPTER SEVENTEEN - EVERYONE SPEAKS THEIR MIND:

Mallory of the Angels continued to present the proof that each event or disaster was precipitated by citizens of Las Nuves against their own people. In each situation, people under orders began to place the blame on God. Soon the calls to blame God became frequent and loud. Then the Supreme Priests decides to continue the blaming of God for the misfortunes of the people. Slowly and surely, the Priests did not take any action to dispel the thought that God had turned evil and had abandoned Las Nuves. Eventually, the people were molded into hating God. As a result of this, Gungulae was able to unite the Priests and declare himself King Priest and ruler of Las Nuves. His first orders is to remove God from speech and punish anyone who believed in God. All the holy men turned their backs on God and began a campaign of destroying any and all who would not follow the laws of Gungulae to abandon God. Throughout the entire time that Mallory of the Angels was speaking, Gungulae just sat stoic and did not interrupt.

Next to speak was Jomax. He basically confirmed what Mallory of the Angels had said, adding that He and the followers of God are holed up in caves, awaiting God's response to their prayers and hoping that Las Nuves will return to the lovely and peaceful planet it was before the King Priest took over and removed God from speech. Jomax stated that he will agree to follow the recommendations established here at this meeting. Esteban agreed to also follow the recommendations resulting from this meeting.

Prior to the meeting, Gungulae had a meeting with his top military advisors and high ranking Priests in which Gungulae explained his plot to capture the representatives at the meeting and negotiate with God for their lives and for the freedom of Las Nuves. Gungulae is positive that once his enemies are captured, God will agree to let Las Nuves follow the course set by Gungulae. Gungulae informed his forces that at the meeting, he will falsely concede all the points presented against him and since God is not to blame, that he, King Priest Gungulae will restore God back to his rightful place in Las Nuves religion. Once the representatives felt comfortable that Gungulae will resign his King Priest position, the trap will be executed.

CHAPTER EIGHTEEN - THE TRAP IS SET IN MOTION:

After listening patiently to Mallory of the Angels and Jomax relate their case, King Priest Gungulae stood up and with a sad facial expression, bowed his head and began speaking softly.

"I am not aware that my own people have sabotaged the water system or infected the planting fields". "I am ashamed to know that all the wrong that was done to Las Nuves were made by citizen and not from an act of anger by God". "I am happy to finally know the truth and I am willing to make amends to restore Las Nuves to its proper place in God's kingdom". "First, let me apologize to Jomax, Esteban, and the God loving people of Las Nuves who never wavered from God". "My next apology goes to God for allowing his name to be trampled without just cause". "My third apology goes to Mallory of the Angel for having to come down to Las Nuves at a time when she is needed in God's Heaven". "I also want to apologize to the entire population of Las Nuves for allowing injustices to continue for such a long a period". Walking up to Mallory of the Angels, Gungulae extended his hand in friendship. His smile is genuine and Mallory of the Angels accepted the gesture and shook his hand. He did the same to Jomax or Esteban. To each of the high ranking Priests he bowed individually. After this brief exchange of friendship, Gungulae sat back down and said " I am going outside to order us food, drinks, and a larger table so we can plan how to change the situation back to the way it was prior to the sabotage and the removal of God from speech". Getting up, Gungulae left the room as the others in the room resumed conversations with each other.

Mallory of the Angels and her Generals Samot, Solrac, and Noel

Chapter nineteen - General Solrac smells a rat:

While in the other room, King Priest Gungulae immediately contacted his generals and made sure that the units are in place to capture his enemies alive. Gungulae wanted to publicly shame and embarrass his captives. After their humiliation, their death will be a great page in the history of King Priest Gungulae and Las Nuves.

Just think, in one day his enemies and God will be humiliated and defeated. As soon as Gungulae was assured that his plan is in place and just awaiting his command, Gungulae returned to the meeting room with food,refreshment, and a larger table containing paper and pens. General Solrac noticed that Gungulae's two body guards have moved towards the door in a move to either block the door, or be available to open the door in a hurry. Gen. Solrac's instincts as a soldier and as a master planner told him that the actions of the body guards are not a natural move. Solrac began to see how he and Mallory of the Angels can be trapped and captured. He caught Mallory's attention and quietly express his concerns. Mallory of the Angels understood immediately and both of them took steps to ensure that they will neither be separated or blocked from moving freely. While allowing Mallory of the Angels to work out the details of restoration, Gen. Solrac managed to signal Jomax that something was wrong with the set up. Jomax moved his head up and down in a gesture that signaled his understanding. Keeping an eye on Mallory of the Angels, Gen. Solrac moved closer to the body guards at the door and asked permission to go outside for fresh air and to use the rest room. This caught the guards off balance as they did not know what to do with the general's request. Outside the door are several units gathering together to set Gungulae's trap. The guards, clumsily getting themselves together. informed Solrac that during this meeting, no one is allowed to leave the room and that bathroom services is available inside the meeting room at the end of the hall leading away from the door where the guards are posted. Solrac accepted the explanation and walked towards the bathroom. Something is definitely wrong.

Chapter twenty - Escaping the trap:

Going along with Gungulae's plan of corrections, Mallory of the Angels, Jomax, and Esteban worked side by side along side of Gungulae. Because Gungulae conceded on each issue of contention, the process of reconciliation on each topic proceed very smooth. Each area to restore God is easily identified and proclamations are issue by Gungulae to carry out the changes to restore God to his rightful place. The disagreements are being settled quickly. It looked so genuine that Jomax and Esteban are beginning to believe Gen. Solrac is in error and that Gungulae is truly sorry of upstaging God. It was very difficult to find fault with what Gungulae is willing to sacrifice in order to please God. Jomax and Esteban prayed that Gungulae has truly seen the light of God as presented by Mallory of the Angels. The process of correcting the blame away from God proceeded without any difficulty. Gungulae was the perfect Priest and the perfect host. Most of the issues are addressed and a proclamation is prepared for each issue. Each proclamation declared that God is innocent of all the evil which befell Las Nuves. There were 387 proclamations completed during the meeting with the option to return for a 2nd meeting if more proclamations are needed. The last task remaining to be completed before the proclamations are presented to the people of Las Nuves is to have all parties at the summit sign and date the proclamations. In addition to the instructions God gave to Mallory of the Angels, God also gave instructions to General Solrac. Under any circumstances is General Solrac to lower his defenses. If any double cross should occur, Gen. Solrac is to do whatever is necessary to protect Mallory of the Angels. God also instructed Gen. Solrac to follow any orders, military or otherwise, from Mallory of the Angels. General Solrac understood and accepted God's instructions. Solrac, being the fine general that he is, did not travel to Las Nuves alone. He brought with him 10,000 combat angels and two medical units. These troops he kept out of sight and placed in a close proximity to the meeting place. These angels are combat veterans of many wars, but mainly in the last war to destroy the forces of Hell. Several means of communication were set up should any incident occur and help is needed immediately One of these means is via messenger pigeons and another is via mirrors. General Solrac did not leave anything to chance and therefore carried 2 pigeons and a set of mirrors with him wherever he traveled. While at the meeting at Gungulae's Temple, General Solrac is fully aware of how devious Gungulae can be. If any attempts are made to hurt or capture Mallory of the Angels, he will be ready. During the formation and writing of the proclamations, Solrac had sent a secret communication to his waiting army to prepare an invasion of Gungulae's temple should any attempt to harm Mallory of the Angels or upon himself. The communication also requested that General Samot and General Noel and their armies be notified of the situation in Las Nuves and come to the planet and be prepared to lend a hand if it became necessary. Now if any fowl play is at hand, Mallory of the Angels will be protected.

Chapter twenty-one - Gungulae attacks the ambassadors:

General Solrac, expecting Gungulae to start his attack to capture the ambassadors, signaled his troops to be within one minute away from the main temple and be ready for combat. General Solrac quietly informed Jomax about his actions. Jomax informed General Solrac that he too has an escape plan, but this plan requires actual proof that he and Esteban are indeed captured. So for now, General Solrac's army is the primary unit to rescue all of them. After all the proclamations were signed, dated, and enough copies made, Gungulae said "I have to go out to the other room to get the messengers that will distribute these proclamations to the public". "I will return shortly" . Knowing that General Solrac will become suspicious if the proclamations and copies were removed from the room, Gungulae decided to leave the proclamations behind. As soon as Gungulae departed from the meeting room, General Solrac, Jomax, and Jomax's body guard quietly overpowered and subdued the two guards guarding the door. After binding and gagging guards, General Solrac, Jomax, Esteban, and Jomax's body guard started to block the door with everything they could find. The big heavy table is perfect for a blockade and the chairs will make it difficult for soldiers to rush into the room without stumbling or falling. Certainly, the soldiers will be delayed in getting into the room. Gungulae signaled his generals to enter the room and capture all his enemies alive. The first troops attempted to open the door but were not successful due to the door being blocked from the inside. Gungulae began calling for his door guards to open the door, but they are gagged and bound and could not respond to his calls. Angry that anything could go wrong at this critical time, Gungulae ordered the door to be blown of the hinges. General Solrac quickly sent the signal for his troops to come to their rescue. Without any warning and just after 30 seconds passed after General

Solrac sent his message, the door to the meeting room blew off its hinges sending wood splinters all over the meeting room. Gen. Solrac had just completed placing Mallory of the Angels safely behind a strong table when the explosion occurred. Mallory of the Angels suffered no injuries. Jomax's body guard is the first defender to engage the troops trying to maneuver their way into the room.

CHAPTER TWENTY-TWO – THE FIGHT ENSUES:

Keeping Gungulae's forces at bay at the door, Jomax's body guard boldly stood his ground and he is joined by Esteban and Jomax. The fight at the doorway is furious with Gungulae's forces beginning to drive the defenders back. Now Esteban and Jomax's body guards are injured and had to fall back. General Solrac replaced them and with pent up energy, forced the invaders back out of the room. Yet, the defenders can not continue to hold back Gungulae's forces at the door. The enemy has fresh troop to replace the tired troops at the door. General Solrac could see Gungulae's smiling face, a face that expressed success for him and pity for Solrac and Jomax. Giving way, Solrac and Jomax slowly eased back into the room with Esteban and Jomax's body guard throwing chairs, small tables, and loose items in front of the advancing troops. For the moment, their actions slowed the advance so that Solrac and Jomax could locate another area for back-up defense. Suddenly, a large noisy commotion came from the room on the other side of the door. Loud shouts and clanging of swords and spears could be plainly distinguished. Gungulae's soldiers, afraid of being attacked from both sides, withdrew from the room to join their brother soldiers in fighting the new enemy. General Solrac noticed that Gungulae is escorted out of the temple and away from the fighting. Where Gungulae went became a mystery. Returning to Mallory of the Angels, he explained about his troops coming to the rescue and about Gungulae's departure from the scene. With the fighting subsiding, General Solrac met with his 2nd in command to discuss what actions will be needed to defeat Gungulae and his army. First and foremost, ensure the safety of Mallory of the Angels.

CHAPTER TWENTY-THREE - THE UNMOVABLE OBJECT:

With a detachment of 10 angels to protect her, Mallory of the Angels met with Gen. Solrac, Gen. Samot, Gen. Noel, Jomax, and Esteban to discuss the plans to engage and destroy King Priest Gungulae and his powerful army. Mallory of the Angels is now the commander four armies, one each for each general and Jomax's army at the caves. The plan call for dividing the war in Las Nuves into 3 basic battle fronts. General Noel will secure and pacify the army and the citizens stationed in all the cities of the small continent. General Samot and General Solrac will secure and pacify the soldiers and citizens on the large continent. Jomax and Esteban, with detachments from each of the generals added to their forces, will secure and pacify the areas outside the cities and continue to maintain order inside the caves. After the battle plans are completed, the plans are presented to Mallory of the Angels for her approval. It was also determined by the generals that Mallory of the Angels will remain with General Solrac to assist once Gungulae is captured. Each general and their army will report to Mallory of the Angels, who is now in command of all of God's troops in Las Nuves.

King Priest Gungulae is not at all worried about the armies that God had sent down to remove him from his kingdom. I am here to stay, just like many successful leaders have stated, I too state "just like a tree standing in the water, I will not be moved". As I have stated many times before, "I am just as powerful as God". With that statement, Gungulae called in his military generals and his top Priest advisors to plan the defeat of God's army and the capture of Mallory of the Angels. "She may have defeated that coward devil, but she will not defeat me" stated Gungulae. Gungulae decided that 5 million soldiers should be enough to win the battle over God's smaller armies, but just in case, Gungulae ordered a conscription of an addition of 4 million men to be trained and fitted for war. As it stood now, his 5 million soldiers are divided as follows. 2 million in the small continent, 3 million in the large continent. His personal army of 90,000 fighting priests is divided as follows: 60,000 in the large continent and 30,000 in the small continent. Although his troops have never been involved in any type of warfare, King Priest Gungulae is confident that his troops will be up for the challenge.

CHAPTER TWENTY-FOUR - TRAINING MAKES THE DIFFERENCE:

The armies were set to clash. Gungulae's forces seemed to hold the high ground, staying within the walls of the cities, walls that were 60 feet high and 20 feet thick. The parapets were made for defense and had a commanding view of 10 miles in any direction when seen from the city walls. The small continent had 125 cities and 1.5 billion people living there. The large continent had 300 cites and 3.5 billion people living there. Each city had the same wall arrangement. Each city had plenty of water, plenty of food, and medical supplies to last for years. Gungulae was sure that God's armies traveled light and would not be able to supply themselves. Gungulae was very sure that when casualties mounted on God's forces, the generals would become depressed and sue for peace. Gungulae was going to show that upstart God just what a price God will pay for in intervention in the affairs of Las Nuves.

Mallory of the Angels was not worried about the troops God had sent her. These Angel Soldiers were very well trained, had great leaders, and were also veterans of various wars, including the destruction of Hell. These Angel Soldiers could fly as well as they could walk. These soldiers have fought in all kinds of terrains and in all types of weather. They were well disciplined and had the best of fighting equipment. The key to their success was that an Angel soldier starts his training at age 10 and never stop training. The Angel Soldiers train to meet various types of enemies and have been victorious from the beginning of time. Gungulae was in for a big surprise. There was no one who could convince him that his numerical superiority would not help him in this war. Gungulae was blind with power and obsessed with being greater and stronger than God. Unfortunately, he had the support of 5 billion people who truly believed in him. Once the battle began, Mallory of the Angels was going to let lose Her dogs of war. May God have pity on the warriors sent into the battle field to fight against her angel army.

CHAPTER TWENTY-FIVE - FOR BETTER OR WORST - WAR:

Prior to letting God's forces march into battle, Mallory of the Angels has informed each of her generals and the troops under their command that God does not want to hurt or injure soldiers and citizens who are innocently under Gungulae's control. The cities of Las Nuves will be spared as much damage as possible. None of the cities' infrastructure will be destroyed. Each captive is to be treated with the upper most respect and courtesies. The battle started on the 3rd day after Gungulae attempted to capture Mallory of the Angels and General Solrac, Jomax, and Esteban. The day is pleasant with the sun shining and birds singing. In what appeared to be an earthquake, the first 5 cities in the small continent came under a quick lightning strike, both from the ground and from the air. The early morning strike caught the troops guarding the gates by complete surprise. The gates are found open and General Noel's troops were able to secure all entrances and exits to the 5 cities within 10 minutes of the start of the battle. The flying angels are able to overcome two small garrisons of guards that were assigned to man the walls of the cities. With quick precision, Noel's troops captured the remaining troops who were either still sleeping or just awoken by the noise and the movement outside their barracks. With the troops of these 5 cities captured, General Noel offered the people complete freedom to continue their lives so long as they did not try to harm his troops. The civilian leader of each of the 5 cities agreed and stated that they are happy to be rescued from Gungulae and his impossible laws. Mean while, at the larger continent, General Solrac attacked ten cities on the southern end of the continent at 3 a.m, followed by Gen. Samot's 3 a.m. attack on 10 northern cities. The attacks created so much confusion that the defending soldiers had little time to respond to the attack, let alone see who and where the attack was coming from. In a matter of hours, 25 cities (five cites in the small continent and 20 cities in the large continent)are captured with no loss of civilian or military life. The captured soldiers are given the choice to be held in holding cells or allowed to go home to their families so long as the soldiers did not try to restart hostilities. The soldiers all selected to go to their homes and families. The soldiers and citizens were not expecting the kindness offered to them by God's army. In fact, the soldiers expected to be tortured or worse. They are pleasantly surprise and pleased. The people on the 25 captured cities are given permission to carry on with their lives so long as they did not interfere with God's soldiers. These people soon realized that God is indeed a kind and merciful God,

CHAPTER TWENTY-SIX - MORE THAN ONE WAY TO FIGHT A BATTLE:

Gungulae is in a state of shock. Without losing a man to death in battle, and without inflicting casualties on his enemies, 25 of his cities were captured and under the control of God and Mallory of the Angel's . He can not imagine what happened or what may have occurred to cause him to lose so many cities in one day. Swearing that this type of military action will not happen again, Gungulae gave orders that 50% of the troops will be awake at all times. Any strangers will be arrested and held for identification. Anyone found aiding the Army of God will be severely punished. There will be limited travel between the cities.

Mallory of the Angels, knowing very well that other sneak attacks will be costly in injury and lives, lost decided to fight a different style of warfare. She instructed General Solrac and General Noel to show the citizens of the 25 captured cities the copies of the signed documents showing that Gungulae and the high ranking Priests have declared God innocent and not to be blamed for any of the mishaps in Las Nuves. The documents, signed and dated by all parties were previously captured by General Solrac as he escaped Gungulae's trap at the main Temple. Now, with these documents Mallory of the Angels began to win the hearts and minds of the citizens of the captured cities. The documents plus the truly reasonable treatment the people were receiving convinced a solid majority that God is innocent and that fighting against God is wrong and evil. Mallory of the Angels, together with General Solrac, decided to release the people from the 25 captured cities and send them back under Gungulae's control. This would do three main things. One, it would Increase the population that Gungulae has to feed and protect. Second, These people will know about Gungulae's deception and share with others their knowledge that there are signed documents by Gungulae and his Priest that indicated God is innocent of all charges and that the harm was made by citizens under Gungulae's orders and not by God, The 3rd reason is that the 25 cities will be empty and requiring no troops to guard them. The released people will be given copies of the documents to share and show others in other cities, so long as having and showing the documents is safe for them to do so.

CHAPTER TWENTY-SEVEN - THE PLAN SUCCEEDS :

Gungulae is getting worried. The army of God has not attacked for 8 days now. In fact, they have released all the captured citizens. He knew basically nothing regarding the fate of his captured soldiers, but unknown to him, they too have been showed the signed documents declaring that God is innocent. Gungulae is stump and unsure of what to do next. Due to the fact that 25 of his cities are captured and under God's rule, Gungulae continues to post his forces inside the cities to prevent further loss of cities.

Keeping his soldiers tied down in the cities caused Gungulae a loss of military intelligence as to what the enemy outside the city gates was doing or planning. Expecting an attack at any time, his soldiers were placed in a constant state of alert which in turn is causing the troops to be restless, tired, and less vigilant.

Once the captured citizens are displace to other cities, they began spreading the word of documents that show that God is innocent and that Gungulae had staged all the mishaps so that he could blame God, destroy the influence God has over the people of Las Nuves, and so he can become King Priest Gungulae, ruler of the planet. Slowly but surely, the citizens of the remaining cities began to see the truth behind Gungulae and his desires to be better and stronger than God. The citizens also are aware of the dangers of being caught spreading this information. They must remain invisible and behave carefully. During the night, the citizens of 100 cities were able to contact Jomax and ask for asylum in the caves. When Jomax notified Mallory of the Angels, She agreed to let the exodus begin but in strict silence and only during the night where all soldiers friendly and loyal to God were posted at the gates. On the 10th day after the battle began, 95% of the citizens of 100 cities departed with food, supplies, and essentials. Once again, Gungulae was furious and punished the commander of each of those cities. Gungulae gave the order to desert those 100 cities and consolidate his troops and loyal citizens to his remaining 300 cities. Gungulae also ordered that no citizen, unless given special permission by Gungulae himself, will be allowed to leave the cities for any reason until the war is won. This action caused distrust of Gungulae and of his loyal Priests. The rumor going around is that the people who departed from their cities had proof that God is innocent and that Gungulae was responsible for losing God's love. Now with Gungulae's new restrictions and harsher punishment, a great majority of the remaining population of Las Nuves began to sense that they too should abandon Gungulae. The question in their hearts is how to find a way to escape and be safe while escaping.

CHAPTER TWENTY-EIGHT - LOSING GROUND AND LOSING THE WAR :

On the 12th day of the battle, Mallory of the Angels requested that General Samot join General Noel at the small continent with the order of capturing the remaining 120 cities in that continent. After capturing the cities, all soldiers loyal to Gungulae are to be placed in holding cells. All other soldiers not loyal to Gungulae will be given their freedom and the opportunity to depart with their families and remain out of the war so long as they pledge never again to fight against the soldiers of God. Each soldier got down on his knees and pledge to God that they will be loyal to God and never again fight against God's soldiers. They were allowed to go with their families as promised. Mean while, at the smaller continent, most of the population received that God is innocent and the word of the mass desertion of soldiers and citizens from 100 cities in the larger continent. These soldiers and citizens pledged their loyalty to God and were given freedom from King Priest Gungulae's laws and given safety in large cave until the war is over. Then they all can return to their proper homes. Some people still believed that it is impossible for King Priest Gungulae to lie to them, but yet, the proof is available to anyone who wanted to know the truth. It became widely known to the people that even some of the elected Priests believed that the proof is legitimate and that God is innocent. On the 13th day of the battle, General Noel sent millions of flyers to each of the cities on the small continent stating that once their city is captured, God does not intent for anyone to get hurt, injured, or otherwise detained unlawfully, and that God message include all soldiers, Priest, and its population if they refrain from attacking the forces of God. If the cities are to surrender peacefully, they will be allowed to safely continue their lives without interruption from God's soldiers. Any city who does not surrender will be captured and their leaders held for trial. Over 30 million leaflets were also dropped over the cities. The cities are given 24 hours to decide their fate. In addition to God's message, 25 million copies of the signed documents declaring God innocent were also delivered to the cities. The last sentences in General Noels communication to the cities declared the following: "Gungulae has been lying to you despite his knowing that God is innocent". "He lied with the intent of pushing God out of your lives and becoming a King". "He demands that despite his false information, you join him in a battle against God and against all that is good for Las Nuves". "Continuing to follow Gungulae in this false war against God, only places you on the side of evil". "Do you really want this?"

Within 10 hours after the notes and flyers were delivered, each city opened their doors and soldiers, Priests, and citizens surrendered. General Noel, true to his word, harmed no one and allowed life to continue without interference. The soldiers were allowed to be with their families. Over 1 million soldiers and their commanders surrendered. Mallory of the Angels was pleased and sent word to God that events are progressing in the favor of truth.

CHAPTER TWENTY-NINE - GUNGULAE FACES THE TRUTH:

First Gungulae lost 25 cities. Then citizens from another 100 cities abandoned their home and property. Now, on the small continent, the remaining 100 cities surrendered and over 1 million soldiers deserted him in favor of living under God versus under his rule.

Gungulae is not forgetting the people in the caves who refused to leave God and chose to live like rats in a cave rather than in prosperous city. "All of these traitors will be severely punished". "I have been too soft on my people". "Now they will know who and where the true power lies". Calling in his top Priests and top Military consultant, Gungulae informed them that from now on, military rule will be placed on every city. Marshall Law will prevail. Anyone not in compliance, will be shot on the spot. No gathering of more than 2 persons at a time. Permission must be obtained to travel from home to work and from home to the stores. Curfew will start at 6 p.m. Any soldier not enforcing these rules will be shot and their family placed in prison indefinitely. This should keep desertions down. I will challenge God or any of his generals to a one on one fight to the death with the winner takes all. Gungulae sent a messenger to General Solrac with his challenge. Neither God or the Generals responded to the challenge. Killing Gungulae and his followers is not an option God wanted to entertain without first trying other means of winning the war in Las Nuves. Since God and his generals refuse to meet him man to man and God's army is refusing to meet his forces in battle, King Priest Gungulae ordered his remaining 1 million soldiers to leave the cities and find and destroy God's forces where they find them. "I will bring the fight to those cowards" snapped Gungulae.

CHAPTER THIRTY - FEAR GRIPS THE CITIZENS IN THE CITIES:

Gungulae is certain that this strategy will keep the remaining cities in line and produce some victories for his forces. Yet, Several soldiers who had no immediate family, began to desert and report the conditions of Marshall Law, the terrible fear each person has, and the strict punishment for anyone or any soldier, not complying with the rules. General Solrac informed General Samot and General Noel regarding these new situations. Plans will have to be made to ensure that the people in the cities controlled by Gungulae

Are not harmed or sentenced to death due to any actions of God's forces against these cities. The generals are now certain that the majority of the people in the cities want to return to God's blessings but they are extremely fearful of punishment if they are caught expressing their love for God. The plan now is to use this new information to their advantage. Soldiers who have deserted but have not yet been declared missing, will be placed back into service in their cities. While these soldiers are back on duty, they are to discover which troops are involved in the search and for God's forces And attempt to communicate with their families to establish a plan that will safely remove the soldier's family from the cities without any harm befalling them. Also, these soldiers are to carefully recruit other soldiers to join them so that the evacuation plan will work smoothly. The basic plan included the gathering of the families of these soldiers and move them to safety in the caves. Then, when it is safe to do so, encourage the soldiers whose family are now in a safe environment, to abandon their duty station and return to their families. General Solrac also has fears. He knows that any well made plan can have areas that may cause the plan to fail or to backfire. Yet, he prayed with Mallory of the Angels and asked God to bless the rescue plan so that all the families and soldiers involve will arrive at the caves with the minimum of casualties. The soldiers who previously deserted from Gungulae's army are replaced in their units without incidents. Once on post, these soldiers began to spread the word to other soldiers that there is hope for them and for their families. Within 2 days, the number of soldiers who wanted their families to leave the city for safety in the caves grew to over 600,000.

CHAPTER THIRTY-ONE - A GREAT START TO A GREAT PLAN:

Although the task is enormous, General Solrac is able to place 25,000 angel warriors inside the cities whose soldiers have volunteered to go on patrol so that their families can be saved from Gungulae's grasp. The angels, who have expertise in evacuating people from cities under marshal law, joined the soldiers loyal to God had opened all the gates and then stood guard at the gates so that there will be no incidents during the evacuation. During the early morning while no moon light is shinning, the soldiers and angels quietly as and efficiently, evacuated all the families of the 600,000 soldiers and safely moved them to save shelter in the caves. As instructed, the families took all the supplies, medical items, and needed essentials with them. The soldiers who were guarding the gates waited till all the families were evacuated then they too fled to the safety of the caves. King Priest Gungulae became furious. Instead of having control of the planet, he now has only partial control of the large continent and half or more of his army has deserted him. A great umber of his Priest have also deserted him and joined the former Supreme Priest Esteban in an effort to remove him from his post. The small continent is empty and all its cities deserted except for a small contingent of angel soldiers who guard the empty cities. Gungulae is beside himself. The war has been going on for a little over two weeks and he has not seen one enemy platoon, or even one single enemy soldier. Yet, his loses are staggering. He must find a way to out think these generals that God has sent against him. Gungulae knows that he will never surrender and that despite his loses, he still can win the war. He has faith that once his army meets his opponents in an open field of battle, his tall and strong soldiers will defeat any angel army they meet. Gungulae smiled at the thought that God made the people of Las Nuves tall and extremely strong. God also gave them a clear mind that is able to solve problems quickly. His troops will wipe the angles out of Las Nuves and send them back to the sky from which they came.

CHAPTER THIRTY-TWO - BAIT THEM - THEN ATTACK THEM:

King Priest Gungulae's army is now stands at 3 million, and as Gungulae still believes, is still large and strong enough to defeat any of God's armies. King Priest Gungulae's plan to recruit and train an additional 4 million men for his army did not materialize because once the war started, he could not get any volunteer to join his cause. At this point of the war, with all the desertion in his army, he can not trust training ay more soldiers until he is sure of their loyalty. Gungulae's top army general named Sangrellae, proposed a plan of deception to allow him to conquor God's forces. He proposed that a messenger be sent to Jomax saying that he, General Sangrellae, is willing to surrender and also surrender the 500,000 soldiers under his command. The messenger will also say that Gen. Sangrellae will only surrender to Jomax or General Solrac, preferring General Solrac, a general of equal military rank. While at this meeting, God's forces will be attacked and the general captured or killed. Gungulae approved the plan and placed it into action. Two days after the messenger delivered the message, a reply is submitted to General Sangrellae expressing the wish of General Solrac to meet him at an open field that measured 30 miles long and 50 miles wide with no cover for anyone to hide. This, Sangrellae felt, was perfect for the plan to succeed as over 2 million of Gungulae's soldiers will be divided at each corner of the field. No one will escape. Gungulae is ecstatic. Finally a face to face fight between the armies is going to take place. Gungulae will remain in the background with his final 1 million soldiers to provide reinforcement or to block an escape attempt by the enemy. General Solrac did not trust Gungulae or his top advisors. If they can betray God, they certainly can betray him. What did Gen. Sangrellae has in mind he did not know, but he recognized a trap when he saw one. It reminded General Solrac of a bait and switch scheme.

CHAPTER THIRTY-THREE - A SURPRISE AT THE BATTLE FIELD:

General Solrac, prepared for a trap, only brought a small detachment of 50 angels with him to the meeting place. General Samot and General Noel with their armies, are stationed out of sight in a north and south position and located 1 mile behind Gen, Sangrellae's forces. General Solrac's forces are out of sight on the west side of the field. To the east side of the field, 2 million soldiers, of the former Gungulae army, are poised and ready to fight alongside of God's forces. These 2 million soldiers believe that it is only right to fight for their freedom and for the freedom of their families to freely believe in God. Gen. Sangrellae is not aware that he is now boxed in from all four directions

Mallory of the Angels accepted and approved the soldiers request to fight along side of God's forces When the meeting took place, General Sangrellae became angry then upset that only General Solrac and 50 angels came to the meeting instead of General Solrac's entire army. General Solrac extended his had and said: "In the name of God I accept your surrender and the surrender of your troops". "No harm will come to any one of your soldiers". General Sangrellae turned red then purple. His veins almost exploded out of his neck. He yelled at the top of his lungs "I did not come here to surrender, you fool, I came here to fight and to kill you". With that, he drew his sword and charged towards General Solrac. At the same time, all of Gen. Sangrellae's forces charged in from their hiding places. General Solrac and his 50 angels expanded their angel wings and flew up into the sky towards the west, the direction of his forces. They escaped unharmed. Within minutes, 2 million men under Sangrellae's command, reached and crowded into the center of the field with no enemy to fight.

General Solrac gave the command to attack and instantly, the forces of God had Sangrellae and his forces in a four prong pincer movement. As Sangrellae's forces turned to face their opponents, the soldiers facing east are dumbfounded to see former soldiers of Gungulae's army coming to fight them. In the history of Las Nuves there has never been a civil war, or any war for that matter. The thought of killing one of their own went against their nature. Consequently, Sangria's forces facing toward the east, stopped their charge, stopped in unison, and laid down their arms rather than kill a brother citizen. Mallory of the Angels had high hopes that the soldiers in Gungulae's forces would not kill one of their own, She is correct,

Chapter thirty-four - Confusion and escape:

With the enemy forces closing in on them and half a million soldiers laying down their arms after refusing to fight a fellow brothers,

the remaining Sangrellae's forces became disarranged, confused, and refused to follow orders to attack any of God's forces. Gen. Sangrellae became restless with desperation, All his plans of victory are shot down without a single sword blade colliding in anger or a single shot fired at the enemy. His troops refused his orders to fight, especially the order to fight to the death. In fact, the troops refused to fight at all. As soon as Sangrellae saw that his dream of a military victory is no longer possible, he managed to escape with only 10,000 Priests but no soldiers. No soldier tried to escape with him. As it was, all it took was the arrival of former Gungulae's soldiers fighting for God to brake the back of Sangrellae's forces. It is a complete and total disaster for Gen. Sangrellae and another stunning defeat for King Priest Gungulae. Back at the largest city, Gungulae is full of despair. He can no longer trust his troops to fight or to remain loyal to him. After commanding 5 million soldiers in uniform, he now has 1 million soldiers under his command. "I wonder how many of these soldiers I really have". He now has only 25,000 Priests who still consider him King. Are they disloyal too? Gungulae called a meeting of what remains of his military commanders and leading Priests. As of now, Gungulae has only one general, Sangrellae, and 3 leading Priests to continue his war against God. "There must be something I can do to change the status of my situation", said Gungulae to no one in particular, yet all at the meeting heard him. "Find me a way to determine who is loyal to me and who is not". ""If I am to win this war, I must have loyalty". "When I win this war, all of you who remain loyal to me will hold high positions in my government and each of you will become wealthy of money, title, and property".

CHAPTER THIRTY-FIVE -THE TASTE OF DEFEAT IS IN THE AIR:

The meeting continued through the night with no solutions or recommendations. Determining loyalty is an impossible task. Men can change their mind as situations change in their lives.

While Gungulae and his top advisors are planning their war against God, the officer who was placed 2nd in command of the army, decided that Gungulae did not deserve his or any one's loyalty.

His lies about God and his cruel mistreatment of the people convinced him that he owed no loyalty to Gungulae. Consequently this officer ordered all troops pick up their equipment, gather their families, and escorted them to safety in Jomax's caves. It so happens that the soldiers secretly were looking for an excuse to Desert Gungulae's army and seek a truce with the army of God.

So during the 16 hours it took Gungulae and his top advisors to conclude the meeting, the remaining 1 million soldiers with their and supplies departed the city and proceeded to Jomax's cave. They are joined by 20,000 Priests who also are dissatisfied with the wrong King Priest Gungulae has been doing to defile God and the people of Las Nuves. The defense of the cities, the protection of Gungulae, and the ability to continue the war against God and his force, now depend on the 5,00 Priest that still remain loyal to King Priest Gungulae. When the meeting ended, Gungulae noticed that the Guards who he stationed to guard the meeting are gone. His mind can not fathom why his personal guards are not at their post. As He and General Sangrellae left the meeting hall, they immediately noticed the silence surrounding them. No one is talking, singing, or cleaning their weapons. No dogs are barking or making noise. In fact, there is no one in sight. General Sangrellae called for his troop's commanders but no one responded to his calls. Gungulae turned white and almost fainted. What in the world is happening. He must have traitors all around him. In his mind he sees himself as a loving, caring Priest who is dedicated himself to be the guardian of the people of Las Nuves, so why is he despised so much? His ego will not allow him to accept failure or to accept that he can be wrong on any topic. His ego told him that he will prevail and defeat his enemies. The plans made at the meeting are now useless. King Priest Gungulae did not feel defeated. Yet because of all the desertions, he knows that if he doesn't take personal control of events, he will certainly taste the bitter pill of defeat. For the time being, Gungulae has only the 5,000 Priest to work with.

CHAPTER THIRTY SIX - PRIEST ESTEBAN WORKS A MIRACLE:

With no military force to stop the people from retuning to their homes, billions of citizens who were living in the caves return to their home to restart their lives. Since none of the cities, homes or personal belonging were destroyed during the war, the process of restoring their lives felt like a miracle. The people now understood that the ability to return home and the restoration of their lives is because God, in his infinite love for the people of Las Nuves, allowed it to happen. God is back in their lives and each person can actually feel God's love and His mercy. There remain only one city under King Priest Gungulae's control. The 5,000 loyal Priest are tasked with providing protection and standing guard duty at the city gates. For the moment, food and water is not a concern. The city residents when they departed for the caves did not strip this city completely of food and supplies. Former Supreme Priest Esteban requested an audience with Mallory of the Angels to discuss a plan he formulated to help seal the end of King Priest Gungulae. Esteban's plan calls for him to have a face to face meeting with King Priest Gungulae and Gen. Sangrellae. The meeting will take place in the city now occupied by Gungulae, Gen. Sangrellae, and their 5,000 Priest. After listening to Esteban's plan, Mallory of the Angels approved his plan with the blessings of God. It will be up to Esteban to persuade the other 5,000 Priests in the city to stop supporting Gungulae and return to God's love. If Esteban can not convinces the Priest to abandoned Gungulae, then General Solrac will be given the orders to destroy Gungulae, Gen. Sangrellae, and the remaining forces in the city.

Esteban is escorted by 100 of his former Priest from the smaller continent and their job is to bring Esteban before King Priest Gungulae. On the way to see Gungulae, Esteban noted that these Priest are not only tensed, but truly confused. While being escorted to see Gungulae, Esteban is able to explain to these Priest that during the war, God's forces have not injured or killed a single person. No cities were destroyed or vandalized. All the people who previously abandon their cities have now returned and are extremely happy. There are thousands of citizens waiting for this city to be returned to them. The most important message to these 100 Priest is that God still loves them and if they ask God for forgiveness, God will forgive them and placed them back into the Priesthood. Esteban further explained that millions of people are going to need counseling and more kind and loving Priest will be needed to meet this challenge. Esteban mentioned to these Priest that 95,000 Priest have already turned to God for mercy. God not only forgave them but He placed them back into the Priesthood To do God's work. To refuse this offer will mean the complete destruction of each Priests in the city as well as Gungulae and Sangrellae. Esteban, after gaining their confidence, asked each Priest to spread his word to the other Priests. Any Priest who wants to get back to the love and grace of God must leave the city while Esteban and King Priest Gungulae in session with Gen. Sangrellae. Within 30 minutes of Esteban's arrival, all the Priests, with the exception of the 5 high ranking Priests in the meeting, departed the city and surrendered to General Solrac and Mallory of the Angels.

Now only King Priest Gungulae, Gen. Sagrellae, and 5 high ranking Priest remained. Esteban worked a miracle.

CHAPTER THIRTY SEVEN - NO ONE TO BLAME BUT HIMSELF:

Not being aware that all the Priests had departed from the city, Gungulae let Priest Esteban leave with his false promise of peace.

Gungulae sat down explosively, almost wrecking the chair, when he found out that the remaining Priests have also deserted him. King Priest Gungulae has only one soldier, General Sangrellae, and 5 high ranking Priests besides himself to carry out his great quest to defeat God. I can't blame anyone here for the Priest desertion, if I do, I will lose these people too and it will be just me against God.

I should blame myself, but I did not cause the desertions. All the traitors have gone over to God's side and that makes it better for me. I don't need traitors stabbing me in the back. What I need now is a miracle to win the war. If I can capture or destroy Mallory of the Angels, I may yet have a chance to save my position. I will probably get only one chance to destroy Mallory of the Angels. She will be well protected and her generals will not fall for any of my tricks. I must find a way to get a one on one meeting with Her and then attack her before she can get help. I can have General Sangrellae to fix a trap in one of the meeting rooms. The trap will consist of a poison tip arrow arranged so that Mallory of the Angels will be seated right in the path the arrow will travel. I will be seated where I can trip the trap and once the arrow hits Mallory of the Angels, I can capture her or hold her body for ransom should the arrow kill her. Either way, I will have some leverage over God. I may even get my old job back and remain in power. Unfortunately for Gungulae, this plan, like all his previous plans and schemes, fell by the wayside. Gen. Solrac, not waiting for any more of Gungulae's trickery, attacked the city and captured every building inside the city except the building that Gungulae is occupying. General Sangrellae, anxious and worried, informed Gungulae that his enemies are literally at his door step. King Priest Gungulae began to think "Am I a fool for believing that I am greater than God, or is it that the army I commanded was full of small brains with courage of cowards". "Ether way, as the saying goes, a commander is responsible for all the good and all the bad that happens under his watch"." I will not surrender to God - I will die first".

CHAPTER THIRTY-EIGHT - NO FUTURE FOR HATRED IN LAS NUVES:

King Priest Gungulae, General Sangrellae, and 5 top Priests are now trapped in their conference room. Outside their room waits thousands of angel soldiers waiting for the command that will end Gungulae's ambition to be greater than God. Mallory of the Angels spoke loud and clear - "Each of you in this room have been given every chance and opportunity to revert back to the love of God". "Repeatedly, you have refused the offer and even tried to attacking the forces of God". "I am truly sorry to say that in just the next moment, I will release General Solrac and his armies to destroy the ugliness and hatred that dwells in your hearts". "No one is greater than God and God shares his love equally with all those who believe in Him". "There is no place for hatred under God's world". "Good bye". At that instant, General Solrac, General Samot, and General Noel with 300 of their fighting angels, entered the room and with extreme prejudice, extinguished their lives. Now the final tasks of Mallory of the Angels is to restore order in Las Nuves, assist the new leaders to rebuild their trust in each other, and finally, rebuild their trust in God. Fortunately, the tasks are not too difficult because each citizen recognized God's love and they also recognized that they were cleverly tricked by King Priest Gungulae into believing that God was evil and that God had abandoned them.

Priest Esteban is elected as spiritual leader and Supreme Priest for all of Las Nuves. His main responsibility is to maintain constant contact with God and to ensure that God is restored to His former place in Las Nuves' religion. Most of the former Priest are restored to the Priesthood. They are happily helping the citizens restore their faith in God. New elections for Priest will be held every two years. Jomax is elected as 1st president of Las Nuves and he immediately requested that free elections be held to form a new type of government that will serve the welfare of the people. He disbanded the army and the marshal law posted by Gungulae. As it was before in Las Nuves, each person will be treated equally with no discrimination. Each city is to be restored to its natural beauty. Each city is to prepare for an increase in population. All is well in Las Nuves. Mallory of the Angels with Her three generals reported to God that evil and hatred has been destroyed, never to appear again in Las Nuves. God, Jesus, Saints, and all manners of angels, including Archangel Gregorio, gave Mallory of the Angels, General Solrac, General Samot, and General Noel a hero's welcome. All is well in Heaven, Earth, and Las Nuves.

THE END

About the Author

I was born in Ponce, Puerto Rico on July 10, 1944. My family moved to the United States when I was three years old. I grew up in a loving Christian family. I served in both the U.S. Navy and in the U.S. Army for a combined total of 25 years. During my military career, I obtained my Registered Nursing Degree. Currently I am a 100% Service Connected Disabled Veteran. I live at home in California with Mallory, my wife of 30 years. I have four wonderful children. I love traveling, writing poetry, reading western books by Louis L'Amour, cooking and enjoying what life has to offer me. I am truly proud to be an American and proud to live in America, the only country that protects the honor of God.

Printed in the United States
By Bookmasters